Three Little Pigs

A Random House PICTUREBACK®

Three Little Pigs

Illustrated by Aurelius Battaglia

 Random House · New York

Copyright © 1977 by Random House, Inc. All rights reserved under International and Pan-American Copyright Conventions. Published in the United States by Random House, Inc., New York, and simultaneously in Canada by Random House of Canada Limited, Toronto. *The Library of Congress Cataloged The First Printing Of This Title As Follows:* **Three little pigs.** Three little pigs / illustrated by Aurelius Battaglia.—New York: Random House, c1977. [32] p.: col. ill.; 21 cm.—(A Random House pictureback) (The Best book club ever) *Summary:* Only one of the three pig brothers survives the hazardous experience of building a house. ISBN 0-394-83459-3 [1. Folklore.   2. Pigs—Fiction]   I. Battaglia, Aurelius, 1910-   PZ8.1.T383   1977   398.2'452'9734   76-24170   [E]   MARC   Library of Congress   78   AC   ISBN: 0-394-83441-0   (B.C.);   0-394-83459-3 (trade);   0-394-93459-8 (lib. bdg.) Manufactured in the United States of America   3   4   5   6   7   8   9   0

Once there were three little pigs who lived with their
mother in a little house at the edge of a deep woods.

The little pigs grew, as piglets do. And one day
their mother said, "This house is too small for all of us.
It is time for you piglets to go out into the world
and make homes for yourselves."

The three little pigs said good-by to their mother
and went out into the world to make homes for themselves.

When they came to a crossroad, the first little pig sat down
with a sigh. "I will wait right here," he said, "and see
what comes along."

The second little pig took the path that led into the deep woods.
And the third little pig took the road toward town.

As the first little pig waited at the crossroad,
along came a man with a load of straw.

"Ho," said the first little pig to himself.
"It would be easy to build a house with straw."

So he said to the man, "Please, sir, give me
some straw to build a house."

The man did. And one, two, three—the first little pig
built himself a slap-dash little house of straw.

But the little pig did not know that a wolf
had been watching him from deep in the woods.

No sooner had the little pig moved into his house
of straw than along came the hungry wolf.

"Little pig, little pig, let me come in," he said.

"No, by the hair of my chinny, chin, chin,"
said the first little pig. "I will not let you in."

"Then I'll huff and I'll puff
and I'll blow your house in,"
said the wolf.

He took a deep breath.

And he huffed . . .   and he puffed . . .

And he blew the house in.

That was the end of the first little pig.

The second little pig walked down the path that led into the deep woods. Soon he met a man with a bundle of twigs.

"Ho," said the second little pig to himself. "It would be easy to build a house with twigs."

So he said to the man, "Please, sir, give me some twigs to build a house."

The man did. And one, two, three—the second little pig
built himself a slap-dash little house of twigs.

But the little pig did not know that the wolf
had been watching him from deep in the woods.

No sooner had the little pig moved into his house
than the hungry wolf came knocking at his door.

"Little pig, little pig, let me come in,"
said the wolf.

"No, by the hair of my chinny, chin, chin,
I will not let you in," said the little pig.

"Then I'll huff and I'll puff and I'll blow your house in," said the wolf.

He took a deep, deep breath.

And he huffed . . . and he puffed . . . and he blew the house in.

That was the end of the second little pig.

The third little pig walked down the road toward town until he met a man with a load of bricks.

"H'm," said the little pig to himself. "Those bricks would make a sturdy little house."

So he said to the man, "Please, sir, give me some of those bricks to build a house."

The man gave him some bricks. And the third little pig set to work.

It was not easy. But he kept at it. And before long his house was built.

By this time the wolf was hungry again. He came along
just as the little pig was moving into his new house of brick.

"Little pig, little pig, let me come in," he said.
"No, by the hair of my chinny, chin, chin, I will not let you in,"
said the little pig.
"Then I'll huff and I'll puff and I'll blow your house in!" said the wolf.

He took a deep, deep breath . . .

and he huffed and he puffed . . .

and he puffed and he huffed . . .

but he could not blow down that little brick house.

This made the wolf angry. He took a run and a jump
and landed on the roof. He planned to come down
the chimney and eat up the third little pig.
    But the little pig heard him, and he knew just what to do.

He filled a big kettle with water. . . and put it on the fire to boil . . .

and sat down to wait for the wolf.

Down came the wolf into the kettle
of water, and that was the end of him.
As for the little pig, he lived happily on
in his sturdy little house of brick.